Zed was dispossessed in front of goal by a lad called Hanif, whose instant strike drew the very best out of Chris. Caught wrong-footed at first by Zed's unexpected slip, Chris threw himself full-length and clung on to the ball in spectacular fashion.

'Great stop!' Kev cried. 'I'd have been chuffed with that one.'

Hanif stared at Chris in amazement, hands on hips. 'That was a goal all the way,' he sighed. 'Where did you come from?'

Chris grinned. 'Not sure, but I know where the ball's going now,' he said, rolling it out to Lee to start their own attack. 'Down your end.'

Published by Corgi Yearling Books,
for junior readers:

The COUNTY CUP series
1. CUP FAVOURITES
2. CUP RIVALS
3. CUP SHOCKS
4. CUP CLASHES
5. CUP GLORY
6. CUP FEVER
7. CUP WINNERS

The SOCCER MAD series
SOCCER MAD
ALL GOALIES ARE CRAZY
FOOTBALL DAFT
FOOTBALL FANATIC
FOOTBALL FLUKES
SOCCER STARS
SOCCER SHOCKS

Collections
THE SOCCER MAD COLLECTION
(*includes SOCCER MAD,*
ALL GOALIES ARE CRAZY)
THE SOCCER MAD DOUBLE
(*includes FOOTBALL DAFT, FOOTBALL FLUKES*)

Published by Corgi Pups,
for beginner readers:

GREAT SAVE!
GREAT SHOT!
GREAT HIT!

ROB CHILDS
THE BIG TIME

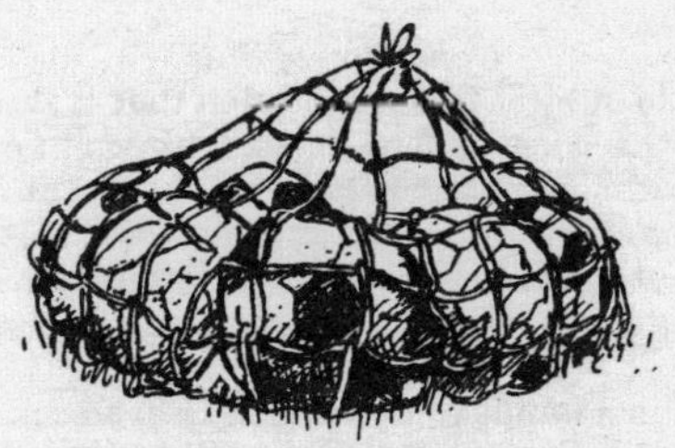

Illustrated by Jon Riley

YOUNG CORGI BOOKS

THE BIG TIME
A YOUNG CORGI BOOK : 0 552 546828

First publication in Great Britain

PRINTING HISTORY
Young Corgi edition published 2001

Copyright © 2001 by Rob Childs
Illustrations copyright © 2001 by Jon Riley

1 3 5 7 9 10 8 6 4 2

Set in 14/18pt New Century Schoolbook by
Phoenix Typesetting, Ilkley, West Yorkshire

Young Corgi Books are published by Transworld Publishers,
61–63 Uxbridge Road, London W5 5SA,
a division of The Random House Group Ltd,
in Australia by Random House Australia (Pty) Ltd,
20 Alfred Street, Milsons Point, Sydney, NSW 2061, Australia,
in New Zealand by Random House New Zealand Ltd,
18 Poland Road, Glenfield, Auckland 10, New Zealand
and in South Africa by Random House (Pty) Ltd,
Endulini, 5a Jubilee Road, Parktown 2193, South Africa

Made and printed in Great Britain by
Cox & Wyman Ltd, Reading, Berkshire

For all soccer coaches

1   Summer Time

'What a shot!'

'Went like a rocket.'

The boys watched the ball disappear into the distance – and then looked at each other.

'So who's gonna fetch it?' demanded Andrew Weston.

'You hit it – you go and get it back,' Duggie told him, slumping onto the ground. 'I've done enough running about. It's too hot.'

Andrew appealed to the other

players. 'C'mon, you guys. I shouldn't have to go after my own shot.'

'Serves you right for belting it so hard,' chuckled Tim Lawrence, squatting on his haunches.

Andrew threw down his bat in disgust. 'Just 'cos you lot can't get me out,' he grunted, starting to trail after the ball. 'I can't help being so brilliant!'

They all laughed. 'You can't help being so jammy, you mean,' Duggie scoffed. 'You've been dropped at least three times.'

'Hold on, Andy!' Tim called out suddenly. 'Here's someone who might save you a journey.'

They followed Tim's gaze and saw Andrew's younger brother strolling

through the gates onto the village recreation ground.

'Hey, Chris!' Andrew yelled. 'Sure am glad to see you, our kid.'

Chris was immediately suspicious. It wasn't like Andrew to give him such an enthusiastic greeting. 'Oh, yeah?' he responded. 'Why's that?'

''Cos we need an extra fielder. Start by getting that ball for us, will you?'

'What ball?'

'The ball over there somewhere in all that long grass.'

Chris pulled a face. Normally, he might well have told his brother to go and find it himself, but at the moment it suited his own purposes to keep in Andrew's good books. He trudged over towards where Andrew was pointing.

He spotted the yellow tennis ball straightaway, luckily, but pretended to continue the search to make it seem more of a difficult task. He wanted to earn the older lads' gratitude so they would let him join in the game.

'C'mon, hurry up!' Andrew demanded impatiently. 'Use your eyes! You must be right on top of it there.'

Chris wandered this way and that, parting the grass with his feet, until he noticed Andrew starting to make a move towards him. He bent down and held up something else he'd just seen.

'Is this it?' he shouted.

'Don't be stupid!' Andrew exclaimed. 'Why would we be playing cricket with a golf ball?'

Chris grinned and pocketed his find, then stepped forward to pick up the tennis ball. 'Found it!' he called in triumph. 'Can I play now?'

'Suppose so,' Andrew shouted back. 'Just chuck us the ball and then stay about where you are. You can field in the deep.'

'Huh!' Chris grunted to himself. 'In the deep grass, he means.'

Andrew kept his brother busy, repeatedly hitting the wayward bowlers into the outfield. Finally, he fell victim to his own overconfidence, lofting a poor delivery from Duggie high into the air. Andrew knew he was in trouble as soon as he saw Chris racing to get into position underneath the dropping missile.

Chris was the primary school's goalie and had the safest pair of hands on the recky. Keeping his eyes fixed on the target, Chris steadied himself before reaching up and catching the ball cleanly just above his head. In one smooth movement, he brought it down to his chest to ensure there was no chance of the ball popping out of his grasp.

'Great catch!' Tim congratulated him. 'You made it look easy.'

'Huh!' snorted Andrew. 'That's 'cos it *was* easy – a dolly.'

'Hardly,' said Tim. 'Bet you wouldn't have fancied it, the way it swirled down out of the sky like that. He was probably looking up into the sun too.'

'Right, my turn again,' Duggie declared, grabbing the bat from Andrew.

His innings didn't last long. Duggie missed the first ball completely from Rakesh Patel, taking a wild swing at it, and the second one didn't bounce as much as he was expecting and clipped the off stump.

'Bowled him!' whooped Rakesh. 'The spin beat him all ends up.'

'Spin!' snarled Duggie. 'Rubbish! Must've hit a bump or something.'

'Who's in now?' asked Tim, looking around.

'What about Chris?' said Rakesh, sticking up for his pal. They were the two youngest boys in the group. Rakesh had only just left Danebridge Primary School, but Chris still had a year to go.

'He won't be bothered,' Andrew put in quickly.

Tim held up the bat and called to the distant fielder. 'Want a go, Chris?'

They saw Chris give a little shrug and then he started walking towards

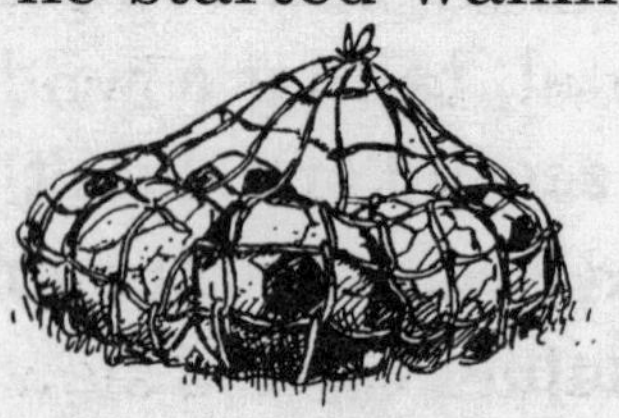

them. 'Sure, might as well,' he replied. 'Andrew can take my place out here.'

'No way!' Andrew snorted. 'Give me the ball, Rakky. I'll show you that pace is better than spin.'

Rakky grinned and tossed him the ball. He'd guessed that Andrew would want to seek revenge on Chris for that catch. 'Can't wait to see you try and prove it,' he smirked.

Andrew bowled as fast as he could, but a combination of a bouncy ball and an uneven surface meant that Chris only had to face one delivery that was actually on target. The batsman managed to turn the ball wide of Duggie and scamper a couple of runs while the fielder trotted slowly after it.

'Don't strain yourself, will you!' Andrew cried sarcastically.

'No danger of that,' smirked Duggie. 'Not in this heat.'

'Just hope it's not as hot as this next week,' said Tim.

'Yeah, right,' Andrew agreed. 'Needs to cool down a bit if United's coaches expect us to go chasing a football all day long.'

'Can't you forget about football for five minutes?' put in Rakesh. 'It's the cricket season now.'

'Not next week, it ain't,' said Andrew, grinning. 'Not for us two.'

'Three!' added Chris from the batting crease. 'I'll be there as well, remember.'

'Yeah, right,' Andrew said, slipping Tim a wink. 'They had to invite a few others along, I guess, just to make up the numbers. Must've been a bit short of goalies.'

Chris didn't rise to the bait. He made his response in the best possible manner, the one that he knew would hurt Andrew most, by smacking his brother's next delivery away into the long grass.

'See you, superstar,' he mocked. 'Go and fetch!'

2   *Time for Action*

Both Andrew and Chris Weston, along with Tim Lawrence, had been invited to attend a summer coaching course run by United, one of the country's top football clubs. It was the reward for catching the eye with their performances during a similar event at Easter.

The brothers' grandad drove the boys to United's training ground, over fifty miles from Danebridge, and pulled up outside the changing rooms.

'Right, here we are,' Grandad announced, unbuckling his seat belt.

'Thanks for bringing us,' said Tim as he and Andrew scrambled out of the car. 'See you on Friday.'

Chris was left on his own briefly with Grandad. 'You *are* staying to watch for a bit, aren't you, Grandad?' he asked, seeking reassurance.

'Of course, m'boy,' Grandad smiled, guessing that Chris might feel in need of a little moral support until any nerves disappeared.

'I wish you could stay all week.'

'You won't want me hanging around,' Grandad chuckled. 'Not once you settle in and get to know everybody.'

He helped the boys to unload their cases and sports bags from the car boot. 'Enjoy yourselves and show 'em what you can do.'

'You bet we will,' said Andrew confidently.

They were greeted by the former United goalkeeper, Kevin Barber, now the club's youth team coach.

'Good to see you all again,' Kev called out. 'Leave your cases outside and go straight in and change. We want to get cracking as soon as possible.'

Chris found himself in a different training squad to Andrew. His name was called out among Kev's under-11 group of players, while Andrew and Tim were with the under-13s, supervised by one of the assistant coaches.

'OK, you guys, follow me,' Kev told Chris's group. 'I want to see what talent we've got here. We're kicking off in the gym.'

The session began with a series of relays to allow the boys to have a bit of fun and build some team spirit. Chris had never even met any of this squad before, but he soon overcame his natural shyness and joined in with all the joking as people made mistakes.

'Not the best shooting I've ever seen,' laughed one of his teammates when Chris kept missing the target after dribbling a ball through a tricky obstacle course. 'Thought we were gonna be late for tea at the hostel by the time you scored.'

Chris flushed with embarrassment. 'My job is usually stopping goals,' he explained, 'not trying to score them.'

The boy grinned. 'My name's Zahir, by the way – or Zed for short.'

'I'm Chris.'

'OK, Chris, you be my partner in this next race. You can carry me!'

'You know what's coming, do you?'

'Yeah, we did the same at Easter. Where were you then? Don't remember you being here.'

Chris shook his head and smiled at the memory of how he became involved. 'No, I turned up at the end of the week to collect my older brother and got offered a game.'

'Lucky you.'

'Hope so. Depends how it goes this week, I guess.'

The gym session went well for Chris overall, especially when a shooting practice allowed him to demonstrate his true abilities in goal. Very few boys managed to put the ball past him and Kev's frequent cry of 'Good stop!' was heard more times than his 'Good shot!' At least Chris liked to think that was the case, even though all the noise echoing off the gym walls sometimes made it difficult to tell which one the coach was praising.

There was no doubt when it came to Zed's third effort, a left-footed strike that swerved and dipped beyond Chris's dive into the bottom corner of

the net. The keeper didn't even get near the ball.

'Beat you all ends up!' Zed cackled.

'Have to give you that one,' Chris conceded. 'Still 2–1 to me, though.'

Zed grinned. 'OK, OK, I'm keeping the score as well.'

Chris won that particular contest 5–2 by the time Kev decided to take the players outside. 'Let's get to know each other's names better,' said the coach. 'Line up by the door in alphabetical order.'

Zed immediately made a move towards the back of the queue.

'Hold on,' said Chris. 'He might mean surnames, not first names.'

Zed shrugged. 'Makes no difference to me. I'm called Zahir Zankar!'

Chris chuckled. 'As bad as Zinedine Zidane!'

'Who?'

'Y'know, that great French player who scored twice in the '98 World Cup Final against Brazil.'

As they trooped out into the sunshine, Chris was pleased to see Grandad was still there.

'How's it going?' Grandad asked.

'Fine – what about Andrew and Tim?'

'Started well as far as I can tell. Andrew's even scored a goal. He threw himself at Tim's cross and did a diving header . . .'

'Save it, Grandad,' Chris groaned. 'By the sound of it, I'll have to suffer Andrew telling me all about it right through tea if he gets the chance. And all night, too, if we're in the same dorm.'

Chris was at least spared that fate. At the end of the training session, the players were bussed to the hostel where Chris shared a dormitory with other boys in his squad. He hardly saw his brother all evening, in fact. Andrew preferred the company of the lads in his own age-group, watching the TV and playing table tennis after the meal.

'G'night, our kid,' Andrew said to him as they passed in the corridor on the way to and from the washrooms. 'How yer getting on?'

'OK, what about you?'

'Brill! You should've seen a header I scored in one of the games. I went up in the attack and . . .'

'Soz, Andrew, got to go,' Chris said quickly, excusing himself. 'I'm worn out – need an early night.'

Chris wasn't the only one who was dog-tired after all the excitement and effort of the first day's hard training. A familiar sound droned around most of the dormitories, as if everybody was practising Zed's name.

'ZZZZZzzzzzz . . .'

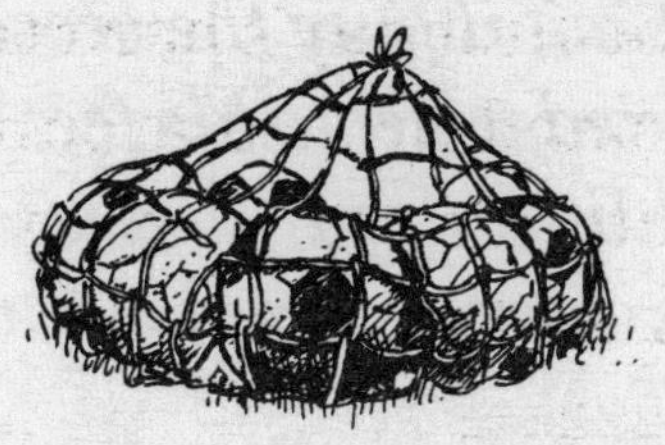

3   Pass the Time

'Ace save!'

'Fantastic!'

Chris waved aside the praise from his teammates. 'Mark up!' he cried as their opponents prepared to take the corner. 'Watch that big number ten.'

That was all anyone did – just watched him. The blond-haired striker jumped unchallenged and his header rocketed towards the top corner of the net. Chris dived across his goal and just managed to get his fingertips to the *ball, pushing it over the crossbar.*

Chris tried to get to his feet but hands were holding him down. 'Ref!' he protested, struggling and wriggling. 'Foul, ref!'

'Shut up, will you!'

'Get off me!'

'Only if you stop shouting out.'

Chris felt the grip on him relax and he sat up. He was in darkness, except for a shaft of moonlight filtering through a window high to his left.

'Where am I?' he murmured, rubbing his eyes.

'In a dormitory, you idiot,' Zed hissed. 'It's not Wembley Stadium!'

'Wembley?'

Zed sighed. 'Yeah, that's what you called out at one time.'

Chris shook his head. 'Must've been dreaming.'

'Nightmare, more like, by the sound of it,' Zed grinned. 'The defence was all over the place.'

'Think I was playing for England.'

'Fat chance of that, not from what I saw today . . . er . . . I mean, yesterday.'

They exchanged a smile. 'What time is it?' said Chris.

'Middle of the night,' said Zed, starting to climb back up into his bunk above Chris. 'You woke me up.'

'Soz.'

'Yeah, well, just forget it,' came the muffled response as Zed pulled up the blankets around his head. 'So long as you don't play any extra time.'

'Who was making all that racket in the night?' asked one of the boys over breakfast.

'Dunno, it was down the other end of the dorm somewhere,' replied another, spreading marmalade thickly over a slice of toast.

Chris busied himself with his boiled egg, trying not to catch Zed's eye.

'What are we doing today, anybody know?' he asked, changing the subject.

'Think Kev said something about watching videos this morning,' spluttered Lee through a mouthful of marmalade.

Lee was right. The players were shown a series of coaching videos, interrupted only by Kev stressing certain points and asking questions to check how closely they'd been paying attention. Then it was out onto the training ground to put into practice what they'd seen.

'Get into threes, lads,' Kev told them. 'We're going to do some work on passing skills in the training grids.'

Chris teamed up with Zed and Lee. Within the confines of the square grid, two of them tried to keep the ball away from the other. Whoever made the mistake of losing possession or kicking the ball out of bounds had to take their turn as the odd-man-out.

Chris found himself in that role for most of the time. He was far better with his hands than his feet and was given the run-around by Zed and Lee as they darted into spaces to swap return passes.

'A bit careless, Lee,' Kev called out on one of the rare occasions that Chris was able to intercept the ball. 'No need to panic. Turn and shield the ball with your body till your partner gets in a position to help.'

Chris was relieved when the coach finally came to his rescue and allowed everyone a short breather.

'OK, not bad, but now let's give you more opposition,' Kev said. 'Try and count how many passes your team can make before you lose the ball.'

The new arrangement was three against three in a larger area and this later developed into a game, using cones as goals, with one player on each side able to act as a drop-back keeper when danger threatened. Chris was quick to volunteer for this double role, keen to get his hands on the ball again, and he had to demonstrate his ability – and agility – almost immediately.

Zed was dispossessed in front of goal by a lad called Hanif, whose instant strike drew the very best out of Chris.

Caught wrong-footed at first by Zed's unexpected slip, Chris threw himself full-length and clung on to the ball in spectacular fashion.

'Great stop!' Kev cried. 'I'd have been chuffed with that one.'

Hanif stared at Chris in amazement, hands on hips. 'That was a goal all the way,' he sighed. 'Where did you come from?'

Chris grinned. 'Not sure, but I know where the ball's going now,' he said, rolling it out to Lee to start their own attack. 'Down your end.'

The save worked wonders for Chris's confidence. Inspired, he could do little wrong after that, and he even scored a couple of goals himself in his team's comfortable victory.

The boys sat in the sunshine to enjoy the packed lunches provided by the hostel, tucking into the cakes and sandwiches to restore some of their burnt-up energy. Perched high on a grassy bank, Chris was the first to spot the bus which turned into the training ground.

'Hello, what's this for?' he said through a mouthful of bread and cheese. 'Not going anywhere else s'afto, are we?'

'Too smart for the likes of us lot,' grinned Hanif, juggling an apple. 'It's even got tables, look.'

As he spoke, the door hissed open and a number of men in bright-orange tracksuits began to descend the steps. Hanif dropped his apple.

'It's the Dutch squad!' he gasped,

standing up to get a better view. 'I recognize that guy with the long hair – he's magic!'

The boys were all on their feet now. 'I'm gonna go and get some autographs,' cried Lee. 'They can sign my bag.'

A shout from Kev stopped Lee and a few others in their tracks.

'They've come here to train, not be pestered by you lot,' he said. 'Big match tomorrow, remember.'

Caught up in all the excitement of the coaching course, Chris had totally forgotten about the World Cup qualifying game between England and Holland. It was due to be played at United's stadium tomorrow night.

'Can we go and watch it?' asked Lee eagerly.

Kev smiled slowly as everyone waited for his answer. 'Well, there are a couple of snags about that, lads.'

They groaned.

'Firstly, there *is* something else planned for then on your programme of activities.'

Lee whipped a sheet of paper out of his sports bag. 'Aw, Kev, you've got to

be joking,' he cried. 'A quiz evening!'

'Right, and I can ask you the first question now. Who wants to go and watch England play?'

All the hands shot up amid cries of 'Yes!' and 'Me!' and 'I do!'

Kev nodded. 'Thought that might be the case. Guess it was a good job we managed to get some tickets for it then.'

Everyone cheered.

'Er, you mentioned there were a couple of snags,' said Hanif when the noise died down. 'What's the other one?'

Kev tried to look serious. 'Afraid we couldn't get enough seats for all of you. Some of you will have to stand.'

'We don't mind standing,' put in Zed. 'So long as it's somewhere we can see the game.'

Kev could keep up the teasing no longer. 'Oh, you'll be able to see the action all right. Close-up view, in fact.'

'How d'yer mean?' Zed persisted.

Kev grinned. 'We're going to choose some of you to act as ball boys!'

4   Time Trials

Andrew and Tim were both involved in a game of their own that afternoon. They had been picked to play against United's own Academy under-13 team to help the coaches assess just how good the boys on the course really were.

'This lot are gonna be tough to beat,' said Andrew as the players warmed up before the kick-off.

'Sure,' Tim replied, doing some stretching exercises. 'But like Eddie said, it's how we play that's more important. The result doesn't really matter.'

Andrew gave a loud snort. 'Course it matters. I never like losing. And I bet the Academy kids won't want to lose to us either.'

Andrew would have won his bet. The newcomers represented a potential threat to the players already at the Academy and the latter were determined to show who were the real future stars.

The match began at a frenetic pace, with the Academy making the most of their advantage of being an established team. They were 2–0 up within ten minutes, both goals the result of well-rehearsed set-piece moves at corners and free-kicks.

'C'mon, we can't let them walk all over us!' thundered Andrew, as the goalie fished the ball out of the net for the second time. 'We gave that ginger-haired youth a free header there. Who was supposed to be marking him?'

'Er, I think you were,' the full-back ventured bravely.

'Rubbish! I can't mark two at once. I was covering the number ten.'

Tim cut across the argument. 'Too late now, let's just get on with the game. We've hardly been in their penalty area yet.'

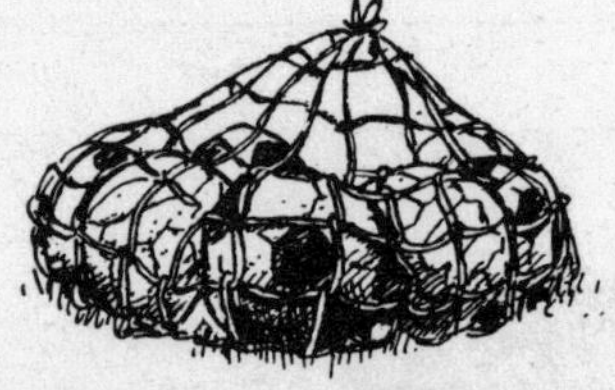

The coaches had agreed to split the game into four quarters so that they could swap players around and Tim soon found himself in the unaccustomed position of right-winger. His marker, the Academy's left-back, was a tall, thin boy who proved quicker than he looked.

When Tim received the ball near the touchline, he pushed it past the defender and gave chase, but the boy's long legs ate up the ground at surprising speed. He won their short sprint race with ease and turned the ball back to his keeper to clear.

'Right, guess I'll have to try Plan B,' Tim decided, having little idea what that might be.

He didn't have much time to think. The ball came to him again almost straightaway and he simply did what came naturally. He used his dribbling skills. As the defender jockeyed Tim towards the corner flag, away from the danger area, Tim feinted to go one way, then switched his body weight on to the other foot and slid the ball through the legs of his lanky opponent.

It was a perfect nutmeg. Tim dodged by to pick up the ball on the other side and sent over a cross to the far post that a teammate headed firmly past the stranded keeper.

By half-time, however, they were 3–1 down and when Andrew was rested for the third period, the Academy took full advantage of his absence to double their total. Only in the final quarter did the new squad find the right blend, with Tim restored to his best position in midfield and Andrew at centre-back organizing the defence around him.

Andrew, it was, who twice came to his team's rescue. Firstly, with a stunning tackle on the edge of the penalty area as the Academy's main striker looked to claim his hat-trick, and then he thwarted him again with a headed clearance off the line. The Danebridge pair couldn't prevent a 7–3 defeat, but at least Tim had the satisfaction of steering the ball wide of the keeper's dive for the final goal of the game.

'Well played, you two,' said Eddie when the coach caught up with them on the way to the changing rooms.

'Still lost, though,' Andrew scowled.

'Aye, well, you can't win 'em all, lad,' Eddie grinned. 'You soon learn that in football. You just have to go out and do your best.'

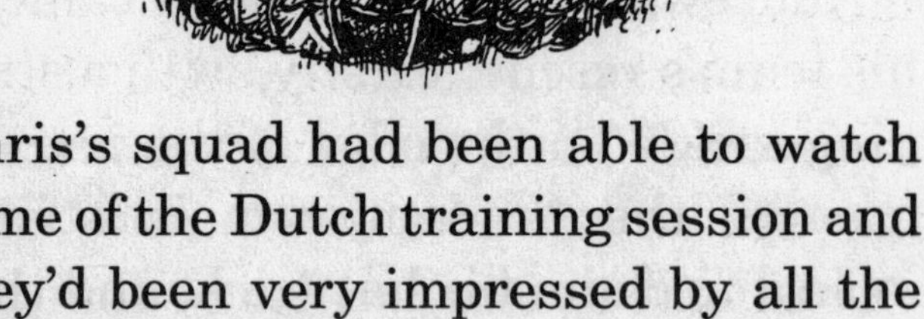

Chris's squad had been able to watch some of the Dutch training session and they'd been very impressed by all the skills on view.

'England are gonna have to be on top form to beat those guys,' said Lee.

'We'll do it,' Chris replied with a confidence he didn't really feel.

'Reckon so?' queried Zed. 'Did you see the way that player cut in from the left past a couple of men and then curled the ball into the top corner? Wicked goal!'

'Yeah, well, guess it was OK,' Chris said grudgingly. 'He wouldn't have been allowed to go past defenders like that, though, in a real match.'

Hanif joined the conversation. 'How do you think Kev's going to pick which of us will be ball boys?'

'Don't care so long as it's not done by alphabetical order!' quipped Zed.

Fortunately for Zed, the coach used another method – a stopwatch.

'I'll be choosing the three quickest pairs,' he told them. 'Find a partner.'

Over the next hour or so, Kev put all the twosomes to the test, working the lads hard in a series of timed exercises based on speed and a variety of soccer skills. The possible reward of becoming ball boys provided an excellent incentive to ensure everyone put in maximum effort.

Chris certainly gave it his best shot. Zed groaned when he found that one of the practice routines involved each player having to dribble a ball through an obstacle course before aiming at a target. He'd already seen what his partner's shooting was like.

'This is where we lose some time,'

Zed muttered under his breath as he watched Chris set off. 'Pity! I think we were in second place till this.'

No-one was more surprised than Zed – apart from maybe the shooter himself – when Chris squeezed the ball through a small hole in the final barrier and then smacked it straight into the net. The goal was no bigger than a park bench, but the ball never

even touched the sides. Chris stood there for a moment, as if mesmerized, until a shout stirred him into action.

'C'mon, sprint back with it,' cried Zed. 'Every second counts.'

Unfortunately, Zed himself went and wasted a few more. His own first attempt flew wide of the goal, but he made sure there was no mistake with his next and then scampered back to his partner at top speed.

'How did you score like that?' he gasped as he recovered his breath.

'Dunno,' admitted Chris. 'Closed my eyes and just hit and hoped.'

'Have to remember that method next time I take a penalty,' Zed grinned.

At the end of the competition, Chris and Zed qualified in third place, with Lee and Hanif announced as the overall winners.

'Right, well done, you guys,' said Kev. 'Your reward is to have some extra training to make sure you know how to do a good job as ball boys. That'll be after tea when everyone else is watching the telly!'

Chris didn't mind that and he couldn't wait to boast about his success to Andrew back at the hostel.

Andrew seemed unimpressed. 'Yeah, I'm gonna be one as well,' he said, affecting a yawn. 'Not Tim, though.'

'What did you have to do to qualify?' Chris asked.

'Qualify?' repeated his brother, giving a shrug. 'Nothing really. Eddie just pulled my name out of a hat.'

5 Time Bomb

The following day dawned bright and clear – and it was to prove a very eventful one for the Weston brothers.

In contrast to Andrew's under-13s, who were working up a sweat in the morning sunshine under Eddie's keen supervision, Chris's squad had only light training before lunch. But then they faced a series of six-a-side games against the talented members of United's under-11 Football Academy.

'These are the best players you will

ever have come up against,' Kev
warned them. 'If you don't match these
lads for effort, they'll take you apart.'

Chris soon discovered the truth of
the coach's words. He was grateful
they were only using small goals as
early shots flashed narrowly wide and
one rattled his low crossbar. The next
shaved the post, too, but Kev realized
that was thanks to the keeper's fingertips.

'Corner!' he announced. 'Well saved!'

Chris caught the over-hit corner and
immediately threw the ball out to Zed
near the left touchline. Zed and Hanif
did the rest, exchanging passes before
Hanif slid the ball home, putting his

side 1–0 up totally against the run of play.

They somehow held on to that slender lead for the rest of the short game. This was mainly due to luck, but also to good defending and two more fine stops by Chris. The fact that one of these was with his feet didn't bother him. He had got part of his body in the way and that was the important thing.

Chris was delighted with keeping a clean sheet, but the next team gave him a netful of dirty laundry. He could do nothing to prevent the powerful opposition scoring twice in each half, with only Lee managing a reply.

After a much-needed rest period, the third and final match was more of an equal contest. Lee cancelled out the Academy's early opener with a tap-in and then Zed put them ahead at half-time by squeezing the ball under the goalie's sprawling dive.

'C'mon, we can win this!' Lee urged as they changed ends.

'Only if we keep it tight at the back,' said Hanif, who had spent most of the time helping out in defence. 'They're bound to come at us strong this half.'

Hanif's forecast was correct. The Academy team switched the ball around so quickly, it seemed as if they now had a couple of extra players on the pitch. But they hadn't. In a rare moment of respite when Zed hoofed the ball out of play to earn a breather, Chris counted them just to make sure.

He didn't enjoy any more free time to practise his maths. The Academy kept them under almost constant pressure and could scarcely believe how they failed to level the scores. None of Chris's many saves, however, were better than his last. The shot took a sharp deflection off someone's knee, but he managed to twist back and turn

the ball round the post at full stretch.

'Incredible!' whooped Zed, hauling Chris to his feet. 'That looked a cert goal.'

The Academy seemed to lose heart after that and Lee was allowed to run clear and make it 3–1 in the dying seconds of the game.

'Two wins out of three can't be bad,' said Hanif afterwards in the changing room.

'Yeah, bet Kev was impressed,' grinned Lee, slinging a towel over his bare shoulders and making for the showers. 'He might even sack this Academy lot and replace them with us!'

'Well, he has said they'll be inviting some of us to join their Academy for the new season,' put in Zed. 'Wonder who'll be the lucky ones?'

Chris was sitting on the bench nearby, a wet towel covering his face. He crossed the fingers on both hands extra tight.

'C'mon, quick! There's no-one looking.'

Andrew tugged Chris down the players' tunnel away from the pitch and into the corridor beneath the main stand. The brothers knew their way around behind the scenes from previous tours of United's stadium.

'We're not supposed to be here,' Chris said nervously.

'I know that, stupid. Just can't resist having another look at the dressing rooms.'

'What if somebody sees us?'

'We're early. None of the players are here yet.'

'No, but other people are . . .'

Chris broke off and yanked Andrew by the hood of his tracksuit top into a small alcove.

'Whassamatter?' Andrew protested, pulling himself free.

'Shut up!' hissed Chris, pointing. 'Somebody's there.'

The boys peered gingerly out into the corridor and saw a couple of darkly dressed figures making off in the other direction.

'Who were they?' said Chris.

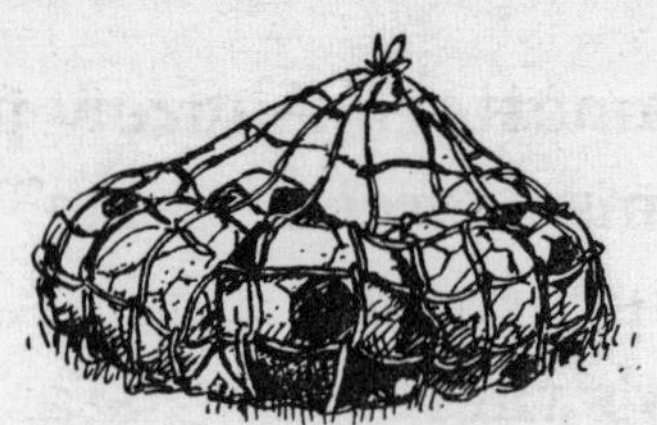

'How should I know?' Andrew retorted. 'None of our business.'

'They looked a bit suspicious to me.'

'Huh! Listen who's talking! Nobody looks more guilty than you.'

Chris gave a little shrug. 'Well, we're not supposed to be here, are we? And I don't reckon they were either.'

'Probably just having a quick sneak around backstage as well,' said Andrew. 'C'mon, they've gone now. All's clear.'

'Think they came out of the visitors' dressing room,' Chris whispered, still glancing furtively around.

'Good idea.'

'What?'

'Let's go in there as well. We've only

seen inside the home one before.'

'Won't it be just the same?'

'Dunno – let's find out.'

The contrast was stark. Hard benches instead of padded seats, fewer toilet and shower cubicles, no individual lockers and cold tiled flooring for bare feet. Even the communal bath was smaller.

'How the other half lives, eh?' Andrew grinned. 'No home comforts here. Bet the Dutch stars won't think much of the accommodation.'

The brothers wandered around, inspecting the more basic facilities, until Chris halted by the far corner of the room. 'Can you hear anything?' he asked.

Andrew came closer. 'Like what?'

'Just listen a minute.'

They both stood and listened.

'Nothing,' Andrew grunted. 'Only that low ticking sound.'

Chris nodded. 'Yeah, but there's no clock.'

As Andrew glanced around the walls, Chris bent down and managed to trace the source of the noise. It was

coming from a small device strapped underneath one of the benches.

'Um, so what else is supposed to tick?' Chris murmured, beginning to feel his skin prickle.

'How should I know?' Andrew said with a shrug. 'Central heating controls, watches . . .'

'. . . time bombs,' added Chris, almost in a whisper.

'S'pose so . . .' Andrew agreed and then stopped. Chris was slowly backing away from something and pointing. As he turned round, Andrew saw that his brother's face had gone deathly white.

No more words were needed. Basic survival instincts took over and they fled. Nobody had ever been in greater hurry to leave the visitors' changing room and get out onto the pitch.

6   Home Time

'Hey! Listen to this,' said Zed, brushing toast crumbs off one of the morning newspapers that were being passed around the hostel's dining room. 'You've both got a namecheck here.'

'Have they got a picture of us as well?' Andrew demanded, trying unsuccessfully to snatch the paper away.

'*England's vital match against Holland was called off last night,*' Zed read out, '*when an explosive device was found in a changing room by two ball boys. Andrew and Christopher Weston raised the alarm and emergency bomb squad officers were summoned to the ground.'*

'Good job for your sakes it didn't turn out to be a hoax 'cos then you'd have been in real trouble,' put in Lee. 'From heroes to zeros!'

'It is believed that Dutch political extremists were responsible for planting the bomb, hoping to gain publicity for their cause,' Zed continued. 'Police praised the brothers' swift action, saying that it averted serious damage and injury and potential loss of life.'

'Pity the game had to be cancelled, though,' said Hanif. 'I was looking forward to seeing all those big names in action at close quarters.'

'Too risky,' Lee replied. 'Once the ground was cleared, bet they had to search all over in case more bombs had been left anywhere else. Must've taken hours, even with them sniffer dogs we saw taken in.'

Andrew had now got hold of another paper. 'Can't understand why our pictures aren't in,' he muttered. 'They took tons of photos of me and our kid.'

'Both too ugly,' Tim teased. 'Probably broke all the cameras.'

'Ha ha! Very funny,' Andrew retorted.

'Did they get them blokes?' asked Lee.

'Nah!' Andrew sneered. 'They legged it away too fast.'

'Not as fast as you two came bombing out the tunnel,' laughed Zed, making them chuckle at his choice of word.

'You've not said much, Chris,' Hanif observed, looking across the table to

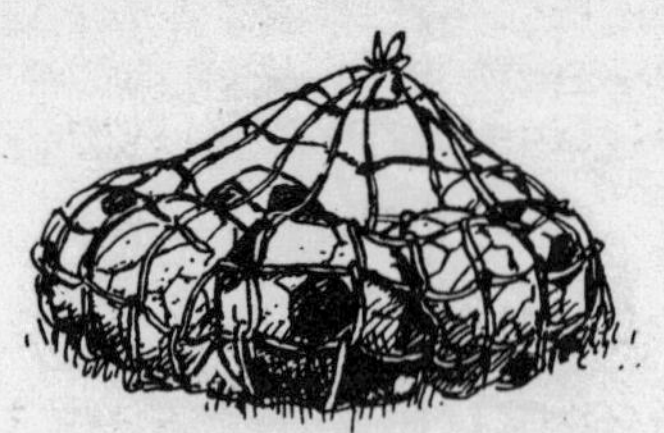

where Chris sat with a half-eaten bowl of cereal. 'Are you OK?'

He nodded. 'Sure. Just a bit shaken still, that's all.'

'Prefer him like this when he's quiet,' Zed remarked. 'He was calling out again in his sleep, keeping me awake half the night.'

'Bet you'd have had nightmares, too, if you'd just found a time bomb,' Hanif pointed out. 'That thing could have gone off in his face.'

Kev came into the room at that moment, carrying a couple of footballs.

'Oh, no!' pleaded Lee in jest. 'We've not finished our breakfast yet.'

'These are not for kicking around,' said the coach. 'They're more for

showing off to people. Here you are –
catch!'

He tossed one ball each to Andrew
and Chris, and the boys saw that they
were covered in autographs.

'Specially signed by the Dutch
squad, in thanks for what you did,' Kev
explained. 'And I'm sure these won't be
the last rewards that will be coming
your way.'

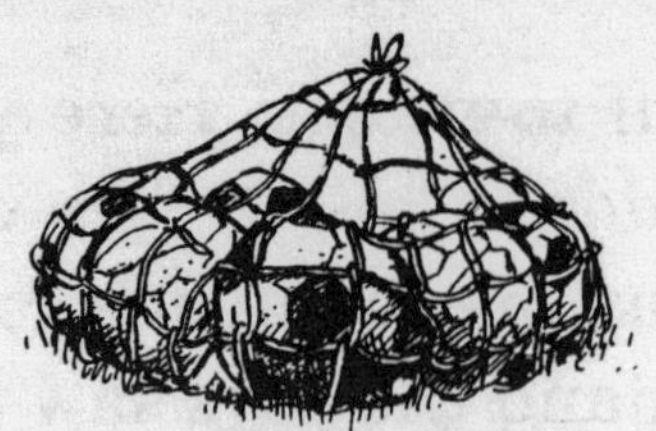

Everyone clustered round to examine the autographs.

'Can't read most of 'em,' said Lee.

'You're not meant to,' scoffed Andrew. 'The best autographs are the ones you can't read. You want to see mine?'

'No thanks.'

'Save queuing up for it when I'm a famous footballer!'

'You've got to be joking!'

'Should be part of this course, I reckon,' said Zed. 'Y'know, practising our autograph-signing skills. Bound to come in useful later.'

'Not for you, it won't,' grinned Lee.

'Right, now hurry up and finish your meals, all of you,' ordered the coach.

'Make sure you pack your cases and leave the dorms tidy before we set off for training. We want this last day to go with a bang!'

Andrew and Chris had to put up with a lot more banter of that kind from the other players during the hectic morning session. There was no danger of their new-found fame being allowed to go to their heads. Every mistake made by the Weston brothers was pounced upon and mocked, ensuring that their feet stayed firmly on the ground.

The final afternoon was scheduled as a series of mini-games, with the coaches expecting to see on display the range of skills that the boys had practised during the week. There were even a growing number of spectators as parents and friends arrived to take the youngsters back home.

Grandad was one of them. The talk on the touchline was as much about the bomb-scare drama as the football, but Grandad was careful to keep out of it. He'd already spoken to his grandsons on the phone the previous evening when they rang home to reassure Mum that they were safe and well.

'Do you know which lads were involved?' somebody asked him.

He shook his head. 'Nay, I don't know 'owt about it,' he replied. 'I'm just here to watch a bit o'soccer.'

'Ah, right,' said the parent, suspecting that the older man was there on business. 'Scout, are you, for one of United's rivals? Hoping to spot some promising talent?'

Grandad chuckled. 'I'm a bit long in the tooth to be a boy scout, don't you think?'

He managed to see both Chris and Andrew in action, strolling from one pitch to another during the course of the afternoon. He was able to enjoy the sight of Chris pulling off a superb one-handed save, but unfortunately

missed Andrew's crowning moment – a ferocious drive from twenty metres that almost took the goalie with it into the back of the net.

'Mr Weston, isn't it?'

Grandad turned round to find Kevin Barber standing next to him. The men had met before at the Easter course.

'Wrong name, but the right person,' Grandad said. 'I'm the boys' grandfather.'

'Well, your grandsons have sure made their mark here this week,' Kev replied. 'In more ways than one. I reckon we'll be seeing the Weston name in the papers for many years to come.'

'So long as it's only on the sports pages in future,' Grandad chuckled.

Kev nodded in agreement. 'We believe they've both got what it takes

to make the grade in their own different ways.'

'Aye, they're certainly different all right – chalk and cheese in their personalities.'

Kev smiled. 'I don't need to guess which one takes more after you.'

'Hi, Grandad!' Chris greeted him as he and Andrew came running up, their final games over.

'Still got some energy left, I see,' Grandad smiled, slipping a wink to the coach. 'They obviously haven't been working you hard enough.'

'Feel a lot fitter,' said Chris. 'Even us goalies have had to do loads of running about.'

Andrew grinned. 'That's true. Never

seen Chris move so fast as last night,' he teased. 'I've always said he needs a bomb behind him to wake him up!'

'Go and have your showers now, lads,' Kev told them. 'Your grandad will want to get on the road before the traffic builds up too much.'

Grandad shook hands with the coach as the boys made their way back towards the changing rooms. 'Hope to see you again sometime.'

'You can count on that,' Kev replied. 'We'll be offering places at the Academy to both of them – and to their friend, Tim.'

The brothers sat side by side on the low wall outside the building to remove their boots.

'What a week, eh?' Chris sighed, bending to untie a lace.

'Yeah, and what a place!' exclaimed Andrew as he swept an arm around to take in the expanse of United's training ground, almost knocking Chris off the wall. 'This is where we belong, our kid – in the big time!'

THE END

ABOUT THE AUTHOR

Rob Childs was born and grew up in Derby. His childhood ambition was to become an England cricketer or footballer – preferably both! After university, however, he went into teaching and taught in primary and high schools in Leicestershire, where he now lives. Always interested in school sports, he coached school teams and clubs across a range of sports, and ran area representative teams in football, cricket and athletics.

Recognizing a need for sports fiction for young readers, he decided to have a go at writing such stories himself and now has more than seventy books to his name, including the popular *The Big Match* series, published by Young Corgi Books.

Rob has now left teaching in order to be able to write full-time. Married to Joy, a writer herself, Rob is also a keen photographer, providing many pictures for Joy's books and articles.

Want to know how Andrew and Chris fared
on their earlier coaching course the
previous Easter?

THE BIG BREAK
by Rob Childs

'*Show United's coaches what you can do!*'

Andrew Weston is off for four fabulous days
of football – on a special coaching course at
United's football ground. It's a terrific
opportunity to develop his skills and, hope-
fully, to impress the talent scouts.

There's just one drawback: an old enemy,
Dean, is also on the course. And the tough,
no-holds-barred striker has no hesitation in
breaking the rules when it suits him – even
if it could lead to someone getting hurt . . .

Join Andrew on his big break in this
action-packed title in the bestselling
football series.

'Highly entertaining'
Books for Keeps

0 552 52966 4

THE BIG SEND-OFF
by Rob Childs

'Off! Off! Off!'

Danebridge school football team –
captained by goalie Chris Weston –
have had a shaky season in the League,
but a good Cup run. Now they face a
crucial semi-final replay – a match
they must win if they are to meet their arch-
rivals, Shenby, in the Final.

Chris knows it's not going to be easy –
especially as one of their top goalscorers
is leaving at Easter and would miss the
Final. But even he doesn't expect quite
so much drama: everything from a
nerve-jangling penalty shootout
to a shocking send-off!

Will Chris lift the Cup? Find out what
happens in this action-packed story
in the best-selling BIG soccer series.

0 552 54639 9

THE COUNTY CUP
by Rob Childs

Each year, schools from all over the county
of Medland take part in a great soccer
tournament – aiming to win the much-prized
silver trophy, *the County Cup*. Follow the
fortunes of all the teams as they battle to
prove themselves the top team in
Medland in this super football series
that combines plenty of match action
with first-person comments, results,
statistics and team information.

Who will be the Champions?

The Quarter Championships
1. Cup Favourites
2. Cup Rivals
3. Cup Shocks
4. Cup Clashes

The Semi-Finals
5. Cup Glory
6. Cup Fever

The Final
7. Cup Winners

Available now from Corgi Yearling Books